COLORING & PUZZLE BOOK

COLORING & PUZZLE BOOK

PRISMA ISLE VOL. I

This is a work of fiction. Names, characters, places, brands, media, and incidents are either the product of the author's imagination or are used fictitiously. The author acknowledges the trademarked/copyrighted status and trademark/copyright owners of various products referenced in this work of fiction, which have been used without permission. The publication/use of these trademarks/copyrights is not authorized, associated with, or sponsored by the trademark/copyright owners.

Published by

TWO REALMS PUBLISHING LLC

P.O. Box 1710, Irmo, SC 29063

Editing by: Chelly Peeler

Illustrations by: Nicodemus Holroyd

Cover and Interior Design: We Got You Covered Book Design

WWW.WEGOTYOUCOVEREDBOOKDESIGN.COM

ISBN: 978-1-955106-19-1

Printed in the United States of America

PRISMA ISLE VOL. 1

COLORING & PUZZLE BOOK

BRIGIT ROSÉ
NIKKI HARAS

TWOREALMS
PUBLISHING

JB'20

SIRENS

SHAPE SHIFTERS

MANTICORE/ CHIMERA

HYBRIDS

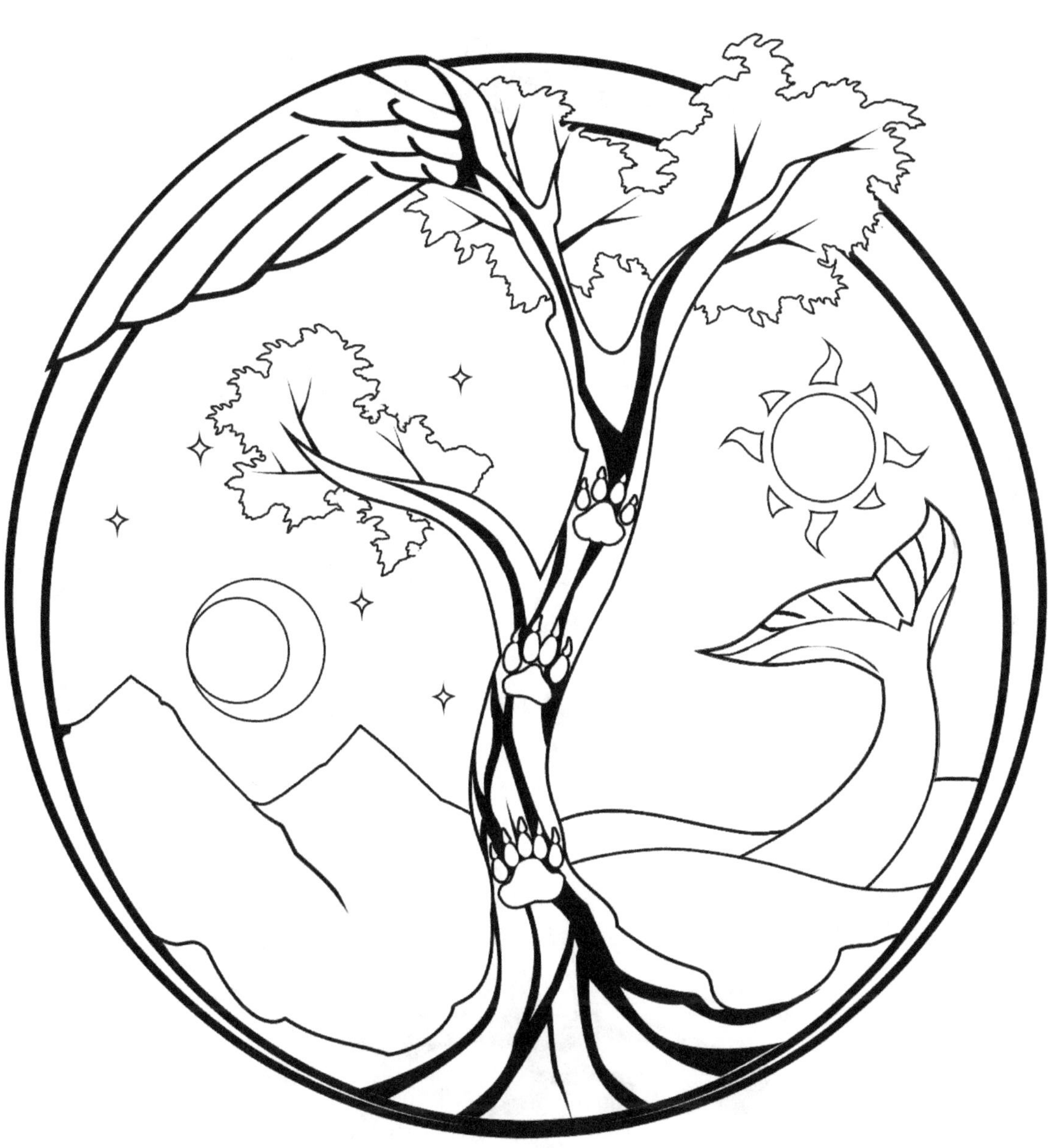

FAE

DRAGON-SHIFTERS

PERFECTLY
PRISMA ISLE
1
RECKLESS

LOGAN & AMBROSIA

GAVIN & PARTHENIA

PIERCE & JOCASTA

MARKHAM

SPOURGIFF

PERFECTLY RECKLESS

F E R X M T G P D N N P L Y K V M P W C X A F
F V M F W I U U C X L Y P X L G V Y K G B J Z
E O G G T M G I M Y S E T N E M H S I N U P P
K L T Y A C P A U Y Q A O O N J K R Z Z W M F
I V M F O R H X S N X A N I T N I G Z E E Z O
O H X G I E C Z S V M S X T S C N D W C G C U
Z K N A N V Y G T U I P Q K O C G Q T A M U L
C K N I P A M E N X H L E I F S T T Z L J T P
W A L X O A L Q P F Y W L O J Y Q Q C P E D F
O E Z J R L W L B X E J O A Q Q X D Z T A N P
F X R A J Q L B E F S E J M G I X C U E H N P
W O D J L I K A V I U N F T N E Q O I K Y V Y
F A T T H W W N F O R V O E R S R W T R B N M
Q Q B A R R I E R R U B O G W E A C T A R N K
V J K K L Y N E G A E H A N D M B M S M I U T
O S H E L D E R W N P T T G B Y Y M L K D K Y
B Z L A B Z P I J I G D A R K Q D N E I O T E
U D H R Y H N G S V W Z O W U E W A P G W C Y
Q M P V R T I O T E D S J E G N A T H B L M S
D Q M O R W B W B D I B E B U X P L J L G M M
P L R U F Z A Y C A G N M B L N D H D T I U N
H B Y H E A C Z H S I N G I N G N H L K Y A R
N X D E V O L E B X F D J Q T R U E M A T E T

- ADARA
- AMBROSIA
- BARRIER
- BELOVED
- CABIN
- CIPRIANA
- DAHLIA
- DEVINA
- ELDER
- FELINE
- GABRIELLA
- GEMBERT
- HYBRID
- KING
- LEO
- LOVE
- MARKETPLACE
- MIGAS VILLAGE
- MY QUEEN
- PHOENIX
- PUNISHMENT
- SANTOS
- SINGING
- TRUE MATE
- WATERFALL

PERFECTLY RECKLESS

1. R A M A A ____________

2. T N S G A A R O A S R ____________________ _______

3. R I G E B D ______________

4. H C Z A _________

5. Y S R U C ____________

6. A E D L E I N _________________

7. S A H R N D O E I R G F T ______________ _________________

8. A I A F G O N _________________

9. F R T I N I G H G ____________ _________

10. A G I V N ____________

11. O G E N S S M E T ______________________

12. S D H E A ____________

13. C A O J S A T _________________

14. N A L O G ________

15. D D X A O M ________

16. R M H A T P E O M E ________

17. I A S N A L O M S L F ________ ________

18. A A I P E N R T H ________

19. P E R A T I N R Y ________

20. A I C C R F E S I ________

21. N E R I S ________

22. E T S R E E H U O ________

23. S L A I V A I ________

24. H H Y S G U R N E S I O ________ ________

25. N Z A N I I ________

PERFECTLY RECKLESS

AILWIN
ARMAN
BEAR
BRAND
CANINE
CROW SKULL TRAIL
DERRICK
DIMINUTIVE BEACH
EVAN
FELIX
GALENUS
GEMMA
GUILER
INFORMANT
LILLIANNA
LYRICA
MARKHAM
MOON
MYSTIQUE HERBS
PIERCE
SABINA
SHAPE SHIFTER
THE FOUR MUSES
TWINS
ZANCLES ROCK

CHAOTIC
PRISMA ISLE
2
TRANQUILITY

DERRICK, GABBY, GAVIN, & DEVINA

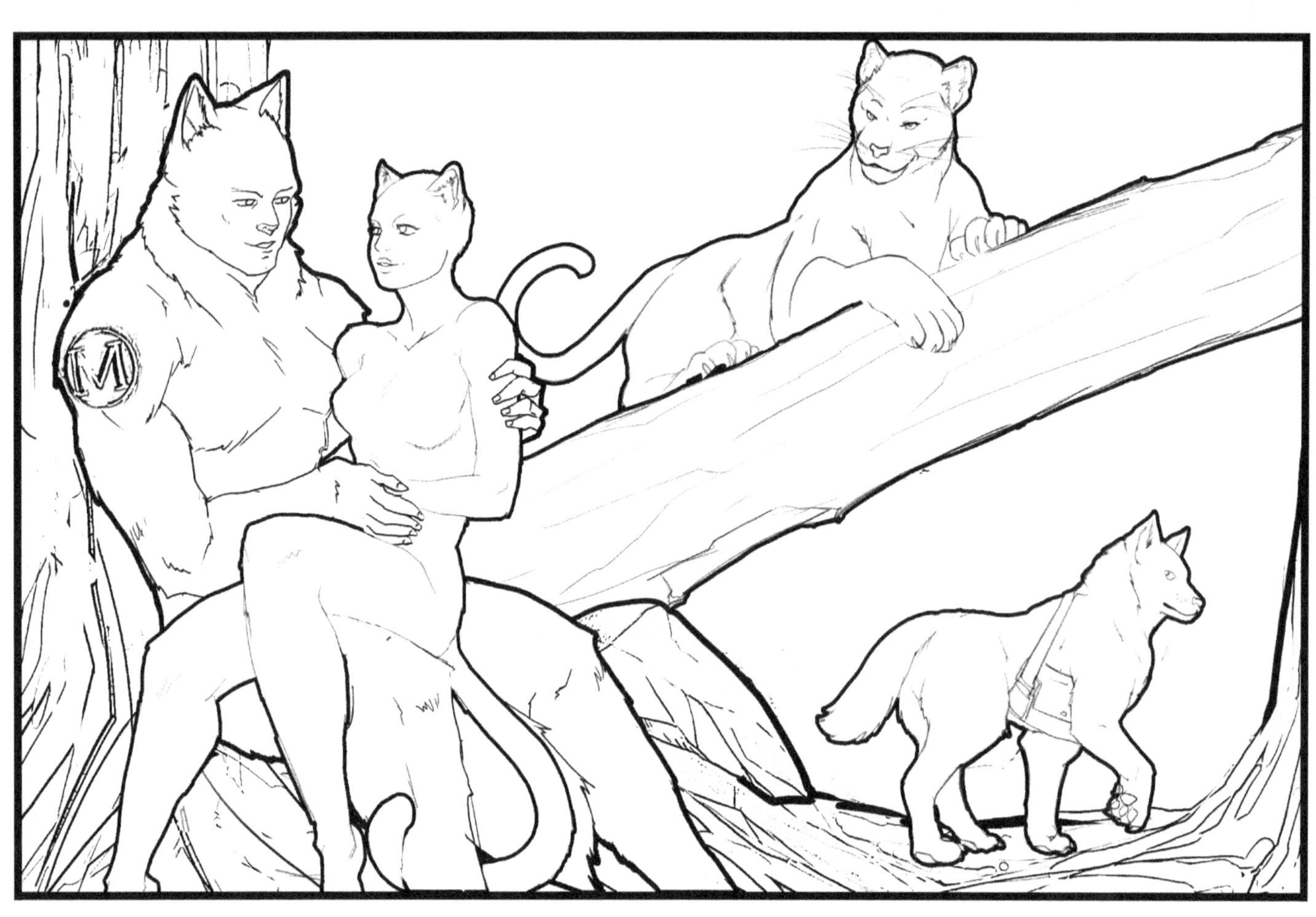

FAGONIA

FELIX & MACERON (MAC)

ALWIN, DAHLIA, LILLIANNA, ZINNIA, PIERCE, & LOGAN

CHAOTIC TRANQUILITY

W V D C A N E T R J X P M Y E X A N D E R V V I
P J S X W A E U M A J O O E Y T L S K U E A D I
Z A W D M Z F I H D M S K W T D A X K O E I O X
F O D H K U A Q P F R X E H O A W L D L T L S Z
L B Y M U W D D Z V X U N T N F M L O X C W L B
L D A H I N D I M P Z M I H F F L O E N Y I T F
E S D R O N T W W I G R A C E O H Q R L S N D Q
V X I C D P E I I S T L K M T D H T E P J B V K
D A P O K I H U N S Z P R E D I M U P A H E S J
R T E M Z X N U A G H N E Q O L B X T U C E Q T
S X L H C F M E H R C F C Z P S D K W Y H L V L
O J W K M D B W S B E R I G M X Q E N S S X E L
X H O P A S P I R I T S O I C Z R E E E F G N N
R W O R C Y R A E I I B M A X A P I Z S A R E Y
W G D O T Q L C M P M A O Z M O L I T L E M N D
G I W P U P V I W G H I Y T D L U N F M O L B L
Q X O H S Z D T N K F T H C I A D U M H N Y E N
A M R E Q X N N R A L G T L B K O U N M A I L Z
W Q K C F N A A Y O I A D T D M S U D Y L M Z C
H S X Y R M M G C N T D B U A X V Q Y K H S X K
D G Z Y A Z M T N S H B I C K T V U Q M I O D Y
Y D F W D L U K N A Z Y R H T E M Y R O C K F V
W S E E B M P Q X Q D E Q K F P A G E O T P R U
R F R B W K W R E F L E C T I O N P O O L S Y Q

- SET
- DUKE
- HOME
- MINE
- BEAST
- GRACE
- AILWIN
- BARDIN
- SUMMER
- TALONS
- XANDER
- HUNTING
- KAYLINA
- LILLIES
- MARKHAM
- MY ROCK
- SPIRITS
- PROPHECY
- WOODWORK
- DAFFODILS
- NIGHTMARE
- CAMOUFLAGE
- METAMORPHE
- REFLECTION POOLS

CHAOTIC TRANQUILITY

1. T I S F A A A N ____________________

2. Y B L L A U L _________________

3. M S E I N S E _________________

4. P S R A T P T A E L ____________ ____________

5. T N H U R E ______________

6. R H S B E ____________

7. N V I N E O S _________________

8. K Y A A N ____________

9. N C R T M G I E A Y O N M E ______________ ____________________

10. D N K I M I L N ____________________

11. S A R C S ____________

12. R Y R E A A ______________

13. U N N L E S T _________________

14. B S I A N ____________

15. E M U N Y E Q ____ ____________

16. S D O G __________

17. N I E C S R U R S E ____________ ____________

18. I B L R A Y R _________________

19. T H R T S G N E ___________________

20. E M R E D T E _________________

21. G T A _______

22. I N I N Z ____________

23. C I T H A ____________

24. R U S C Y ____________

25. T P G R N N A E ___________________

CHAOTIC TRANQUILITY

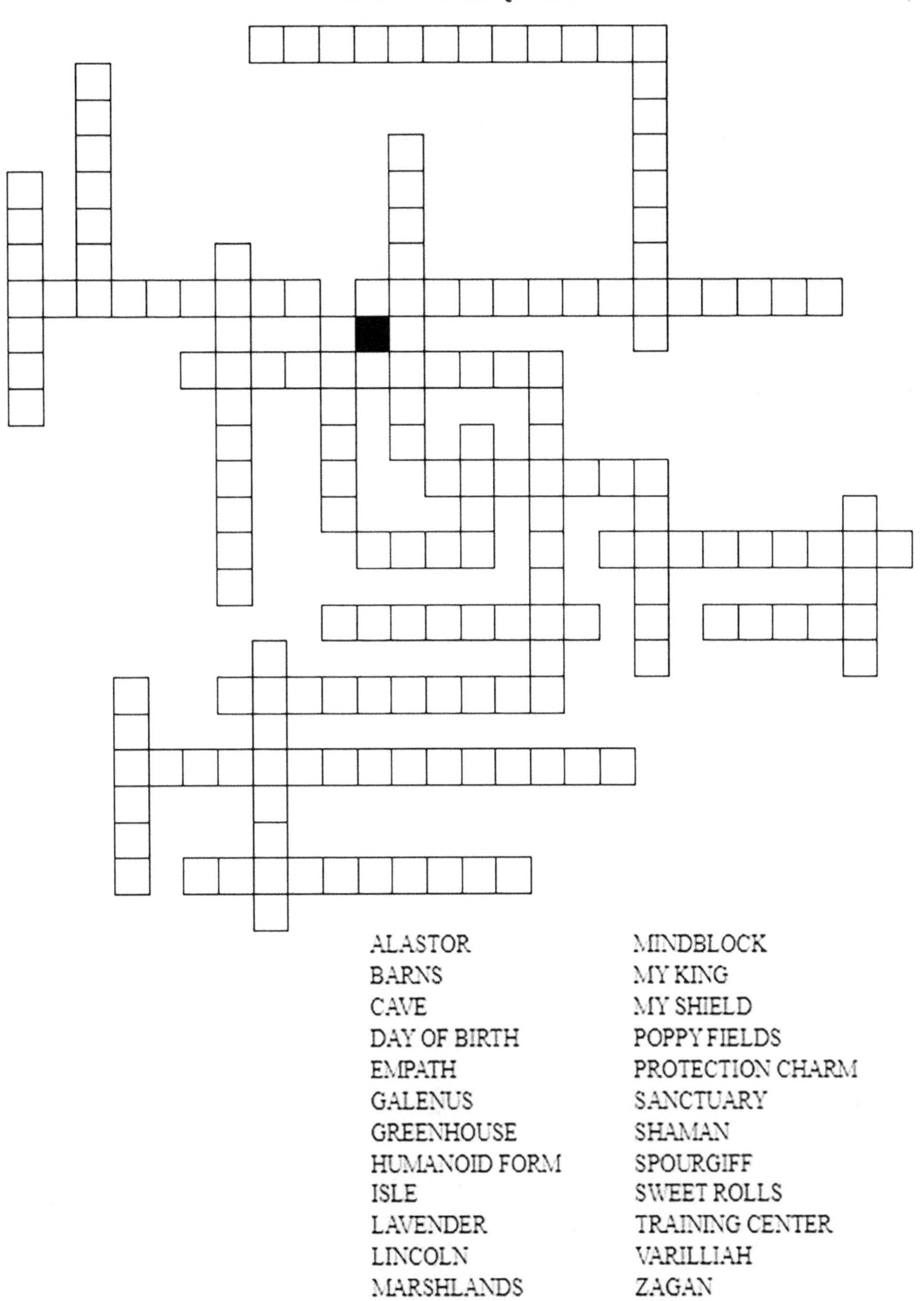

DARKNESS RECONCILED PREVIEW

PRISMA ISLE BOOK 7

BY BRIGIT ROSÉ & NIKKI HARAS

Jocasta stared off as Pierce carried her up the staircase into their home. Not that it quite felt that way. Her gaze flicked from one lackluster room to the next. A few things had fallen onto the floor, but nothing appeared broken. It seemed like a dream that had twisted into a nightmare she couldn't wake up from.

Hey, are you okay? She heard her sister's voice in her head.

Without peering at Ambrosia over Pierce's shoulder, Jo simply responded, *Yeah. I'm just shaken, I guess.* If it hadn't been for Adara, neither she nor her and Pierce's unborn child would still be here. A broken leg didn't compare to the price Adara had paid to keep them safe.

"Should I just set these here?" Logan held the crutches up as he lingered by the door.

Uncertain Pierce would've heard the question, especially as she didn't know how long before the ringing in his ears would clear up, Jo answered, "That's fine, I guess." They could always move them later, right?

Pierce glanced around and looked down at her. "Would you like to lie on the couch or in bed?"

"The bed is fine." It was better than the couch. Her gaze flicked to the rattle still in her hand, something she'd worked on with Adara's help for over a week. Yet all she could think about was how he hadn't even bothered to glance at the sonogram. Not once had his eyes lifted. It had been nearly three weeks since they found out she was pregnant. Three weeks of him becoming more and more distant. No matter how much he appeared to be present, it had only become even more apparent that she wouldn't be able to reach him. Not that she had any idea what to do anymore, except for one thing. "Am, can you actually bring my crutches into the bedroom?"

"Uh, yeah," Ambrosia replied. "Why don't you go check on Zinnia and Lilli? I'll hang here with them," she said to Logan.

"Are you sure?" he asked.

"I'm positive."

"All right." Leaning down, he gave her a quick kiss and left.

Pierce peered over his shoulder in time to see the front door close. Facing forward, he carried her down the hall into their bedroom and got her settled carefully and gently in the bed. "Do you want to change?"

Nothing. Her mate just stood there, staring at her. Did anything even register with him anymore? She couldn't tell, his expression didn't change. Jo eyed her clothes. Dust covered most of her dress, and crimson stained the collar. She should change, but she could barely stand to look at him. Not when he looked like her mate but felt like a stranger. If it hadn't been for his ears, she wouldn't have lifted her eyes to him, but he had to see her mouth to read it. "Ambrosia can help me."

"If you are sure." Pierce paused. "I know you cannot get your cast wet, but would you like me to run some warm water so you can wash?"

"No. Right now, I just want to change clothes and lie down." So she could figure out what to do next because she didn't know. Not when they only went through the motions. He acted like an attentive mate, and she pretended nothing was wrong; as if she still knew him and didn't feel alone. All of which was the furthest from the truth. As much as she wanted to believe the male she'd fallen in love with was still in there somewhere, she didn't know how to believe it when he'd gotten so far out of reach.

He gave a quick nod. "What about some tea or something to eat? You need to eat."

Right. She and Adara had started for some place for lunch when…tears welled in the corners of her eyes and trickled down her cheeks. "Uh, yeah." Jo dropped her gaze to the bedding and sent a telepathic message to her sister. *Has someone reached out to Adara's daughters?*

Yes, we've ensured someone passed the information along and retrieved her body, her sister replied.

Good. That wasn't something she could handle doing herself.

"I will make you some of that herbal tea," her mate said. "What would you like to eat?"

Really, she needed to eat. Jo flicked her gaze back to him. "I don't care." As much as she had to think about their unborn child, her mind kept going back to Adara and everything the female had done for them.

"Okay. I will be back soon with something, then."

Jo didn't even bother watching as he walked out of their bedroom. More tears rolled down her face. Gods, why couldn't she stop crying?

"Hey," Ambrosia said as she closed the door.

She half-turned her attention to her sister who crossed the room, sat on the bed, and embraced her. "I just want it to stop," Jo whispered as she wrapped her arms tightly around her sister.

"I know."

Sobbing harder, Jo tightened the hold she had on the female. Her heart broke. She was to blame for what happened. Adara had been in the bar because *she* wanted to make Pierce something that might snap him out of this. And it hadn't done a damn thing except cost Adara her life. That just made her feel worse.

Ambrosia rubbed slow circles across her back. "Listen to me, you and the baby are okay. Adara kept you safe because she cared about you. Now, we'll do everything we can for her daughters."

Though her sister meant well, the words didn't do much to comfort her. How could they when one thing piled onto another? Her family had abandoned her. Until today, none of them had spoken to her in weeks, and her mate might as well have fallen out of love with her. This pregnancy was supposed to be a good thing, yet it felt like it ruined everything. Not that she said any of that. Jo released the hold she had on Ambrosia and wiped at her face. However, the tears didn't ebb at all. "Can you help me change clothes?"

"Yeah. I can do that. Do you want pajamas or just fresh clothes?"

"Fresh clothes." At some point, she'd want to take a shower. Right now, all she cared about was a dress that wasn't covered in dust particles, and the gods knew what else.

"All right." Ambrosia stood, headed to the closet, and dug out a simple white dress with orange flowers all over it and spaghetti straps. "Will this work?"

"It's fine." As her sister helped her change, she couldn't stop looking around her and Pierce's bedroom. The only sign of damage appeared to be the picture of them from their mating day that had hung on the wall. She didn't see it at first, at least not until the shattered glass on the floor caught her eye. It seemed ironic how much it symbolized their current relationship—broken and in pieces.

Ambrosia glanced over her shoulder as she got to her feet. "I'll get that cleaned up."

Before Jo could object, Ambrosia left the room. Right, a broken leg meant she was helpless and incapable of even the smallest of tasks. Resting a hand on her lower belly, she rolled over to her side and stared at the portrait of her and Pierce. They'd been so happy, so in love. It was hard to believe only a few months had passed since that day. Now, all she could think about was what if she never got him back? What if he stayed like this?

Lying there quietly sobbing, she listened as Pierce put their home back in order and then returned to the kitchen. It didn't sound any different than this morning. The noises represented a mate dedicated to the joy and health of her and their unborn child. It was a lie they'd become adept at hiding. One that only increased the size of the hole in her heart.

Because no matter how hard she focused, she couldn't breach the emotional walls he'd put up. He had shut her out. If having to dig her out of the rubble, even facing the possibility that she could've been killed, couldn't reach him…nothing would. He didn't leave her much choice in what to do next.

Her sister appeared in her line of sight. Jo watched Ambrosia clean up the broken shards from the floor, then carefully pick up the picture frame, which was now utterly void of glass. "I'll see about getting this fixed for you. Okay?"

"Sure," Jo agreed, only because she didn't have the energy to argue. Her gaze shifted from the mess to the cast on her leg. Antonia said to return in a few days. That's how long she'd give Pierce. If she had to face raising their child alone, then it would be easier if it was somewhere that at least felt like home.

Ambrosia got the last of the glass from the floor and dumped it into the trashcan. She set the broom and dustpan aside and then crossed back to the bed. "All right, I'm going to adjust the pillows here, plus get your leg propped up."

"You always took such good care of me." Jo offered her sister a faint smile. Things her sister knew because they'd done it before. All things she could've told her mate, but how much of it would he have understood? Not that his ears would be that way forever, but that didn't impact everything else.

"Yeah, well, I'd really like it if we could quit doing this."

"I'll do my best," she replied as Ambrosia got pillows propped up against her back and under her leg.

Pierce entered the bedroom with a tray of food in hand. The scent of oven-roasted chicken wafted through the air. Shifting the tray to one hand, he slid the lantern over before setting the tray on the bedside table. "Here you go. Is this okay?"

Her eyes flipped from the chicken slices to the vegetables, the fruit, and the rice. Before she could say anything, her stomach rumbled. That probably said more than she'd utter with her words. It all looked delectable.

"Guess that answers that question," Ambrosia joked.

Yeah, it did. Jo just nodded. If nothing else, she could at least be polite. Maybe she couldn't feel the emotions going through him, maybe he had shut down, but he still tried to be here, even in a small way. Not that it eased her feelings, but it was better than him not being here at all. And it didn't change that she feared how far things would fall between them, because she couldn't handle things getting worse. "Yes, thank you."

Pierce gave a slight nod, turned, and left. Jo stared after him as he disappeared into the kitchen, likely to clean up whatever mess he'd made preparing her meal.

"Can you get that into your lap? Or do you have another tray that'll work better?" her sister asked as she picked up the picture, plus the broom and dustpan.

"I can get to this just fine." She didn't need any special treatment. This was more than she deserved.

"All right." Without arguing or questioning things further, Ambrosia started to leave but stopped just in the doorway. *Are you sure you're okay?*

Taking the fruit bowl in her hand, Jo put a piece in her mouth and considered her sister's telepathic question. It was something Ambrosia could've asked aloud, but she knew why the female hadn't done that. *I'm alive. We're both alive. I'm grateful for that, but I feel guilty.*

You have no reason to feel that way, though I understand. That wasn't what I meant, and you know it.

Yes, she did, and she'd purposely avoided answering it. "I'm fine," Jo mumbled before stuffing another piece of fruit in her mouth.

Ambrosia let out a heavy sigh. "All right." Without another word, she headed down the hall.

Picking at the fruit, Jo watched as her sister returned the broom and dustpan to the closet and then stopped just outside the kitchen.

"Pierce," Ambrosia called out.

Jo leaned back and peered down the hallway. She could see her sister, who had failed to get her mate's attention. It didn't surprise her as she'd seen Antonia purposely put herself in his line of sight. She considered offering her sister some advice for a moment, but she doubted the female required it.

"Pierce," Ambrosia repeated, louder this time, as she slapped her hand on the kitchen counter.

Nope. Just as she thought. It looked like it worked this time.

"The frame that held your mating day picture on the wall broke. I cleaned it up, and I'm taking what's left of it to have it fixed," Ambrosia said.

"Okay. Thank you."

"Um, yeah, you're welcome." With a slight shake of her head, she strode toward the front door.

Three words; her mate only uttered three words. Jo watched her sister leave and then refocused on her food. It was pointless to do anything else. She finished the last of the fruit, placed the empty bowl on the tray, and selected the plate of chicken next. Jo paused with her fork buried in the chicken. Listening to Pierce's footsteps, she peered down the hall just as a chair at their dining room table slid across the floor. The movement around their kitchen told her he'd worked on food for himself, not to mention the aromas that filled their home. He sat at the table instead of eating in the bedroom with her. Fresh tears trickled down her cheeks. Gods, she was an idiot.

"I'm so sorry," she whispered to their unborn child. While her tears didn't subside, Jo forced herself to finish eating and drank about half of the mug of tea. She didn't bother calling out to her mate. He wouldn't hear her, anyway. Though she suspected he might check on things at some point, at least in theory. Rolling over to her side, she turned her back to their bedroom door, wrapped her arms around herself, and whimpered.

"Would you like me to leave the tea?"

She didn't even bother trying to vocalize a response. Instead, she just shook her head. Because to say something meant she'd have to look at him, and she couldn't bear that, not when an expressionless face was all that would greet her. Yes, he likely smelled her tears, but that didn't mean they affected him. Not in the way they used to do.

"I will take care of your dishes, then. Do you need anything else?"

Again, she just shook her head. The only thing she needed was close yet entirely out of reach at the same time. There was no point in even asking for it.

"Okay." Pierce picked up her tray and left the bedroom.

A one-word answer. They had indeed become strangers in their own home. She didn't know what happened to him, not that he'd tell her. He hadn't told her a few weeks ago when he requested time, which she'd given him in spades. But she couldn't keep doing it, especially as it only caused her more pain. Jo fixed her gaze on the rattle she'd set on the bed—only one option stared her in the face.

Once her leg healed, she'd do what was necessary for their child.

And leave.

REBEL
TIDES
PRISMA ISLE
3

THALASIA

AURELIA

BRUCE, CORA, & CARSON

REBEL TIDES

I E A Y J V C I A W R X V F S K K O S S I
G J Y N F Y I A X Q V M G E F C X E J T U
N N O E B H F N Y W I F N H X F I T J A T
T Q G X Y F F C N A S O E C Y R C F M I A
E T K U E W E M S K M H X L I U H A T R B
N Y M M I H L E A O E Z W A I E I X S W I
E H I A P L L E R N M E F E A X C F R A G
Q U S O H A E E P C T N P O J E A C D Y A
U I R S C R H R I R P I R E G I N A J T R
K P Y S O P B L N X E O C S R S E V N O M
E F L E J S L F R S B C H O C J V V R H Y
Y D A T P O Q E E F X P H V R R I G N E P
Q R Z O R F P Y D C Y R C A P E L W G A Q
T A V T X E E U S L N H P Z U P L H A V V
Z K S K E R R Z G O H P B H S N A O J E E
I E X K E R Z E R S Y E S R F E G A V N R
R S R V W W X E D S O P C C I V E T H J I
K A L W E N C H A N T R E S S D W Q T Z E
B I K T X A R W R O C Y N R I C G P J B X
S B U R M Q T Z B P J I P W T V E E O S B
N X E T D V P R C O L L A R I T Q B E Y V

- ARMY
- BARKEEPER
- BRIDGE
- CHICANE VILLAGE
- COLLAR
- CYNRIC
- DRAKES
- ENCHANTRESS
- FAIRIES
- FELIX
- GLYPHS
- GUILER
- INNKEEPER
- KEY
- LEPRECHAUN
- MACERON
- MANTICORE
- PHEROMONES
- PROPHECY
- REGINA
- SCALES
- SILVER EYES
- STAIRWAY TO HEAVEN
- TROLL
- VERIE

REBEL TIDES

1. B T A A E N S I S T ________ ________

2. S E C N A C L O R K Z ____________ _______

3. O F L C S A D D N L O U _______ ___ __________

4. G M I A C ________

5. A E R V _______

6. E N G T E R __________

7. U E L A A I R ____________

8. K Y M E E S P T L _____ __________

9. G E L I N S R D G O N T S __________ ____________

10. T O D H N A B R U E _________________

11. E Y L R _______

12. G D L D I E __________

13. A O I H D N U M ______________

14. O S E P N R I R ____________________

15. M E I A R K _______________

16. O H E C N ____________

17. Y A K O K E C E O K A J R _________________ _______________

18. S E E T A S R F H P I H ____________ _________________

19. R W I U C A T L R S K L L O __________ ____________ ____________

20. V E I N I H C U B T E D I A M _________________________ ____________

21. L D U O C C T R O U ____________ ____________

22. K O B O __________

23. S A H L I T A A ____________________

24. E A F E S R T H ____________________

25. T A Y T A L C S ____________________

REBEL TIDES

- CANDESCENT ISLE
- DRAGON SHIFTER
- LOTUS BLOSSOMS
- ENGRAVINGS
- LAKE LUCENT
- HALF BREED
- MATRIARCH
- SAFE JUICE
- CREATURE
- FOUNTAIN
- GREAT WAR
- BARRIER
- CHIMERA
- DEMETER
- JAERIKO
- VISIONS
- MAGGIE
- TALONS
- ATLIS
- FANGS
- SIREN
- WINGS
- SERU

SIREN'S
CURSE
PRISMA ISLE
4

CIPRIANA & PARTHENIA

THALASIA & SERU

LUCIEL

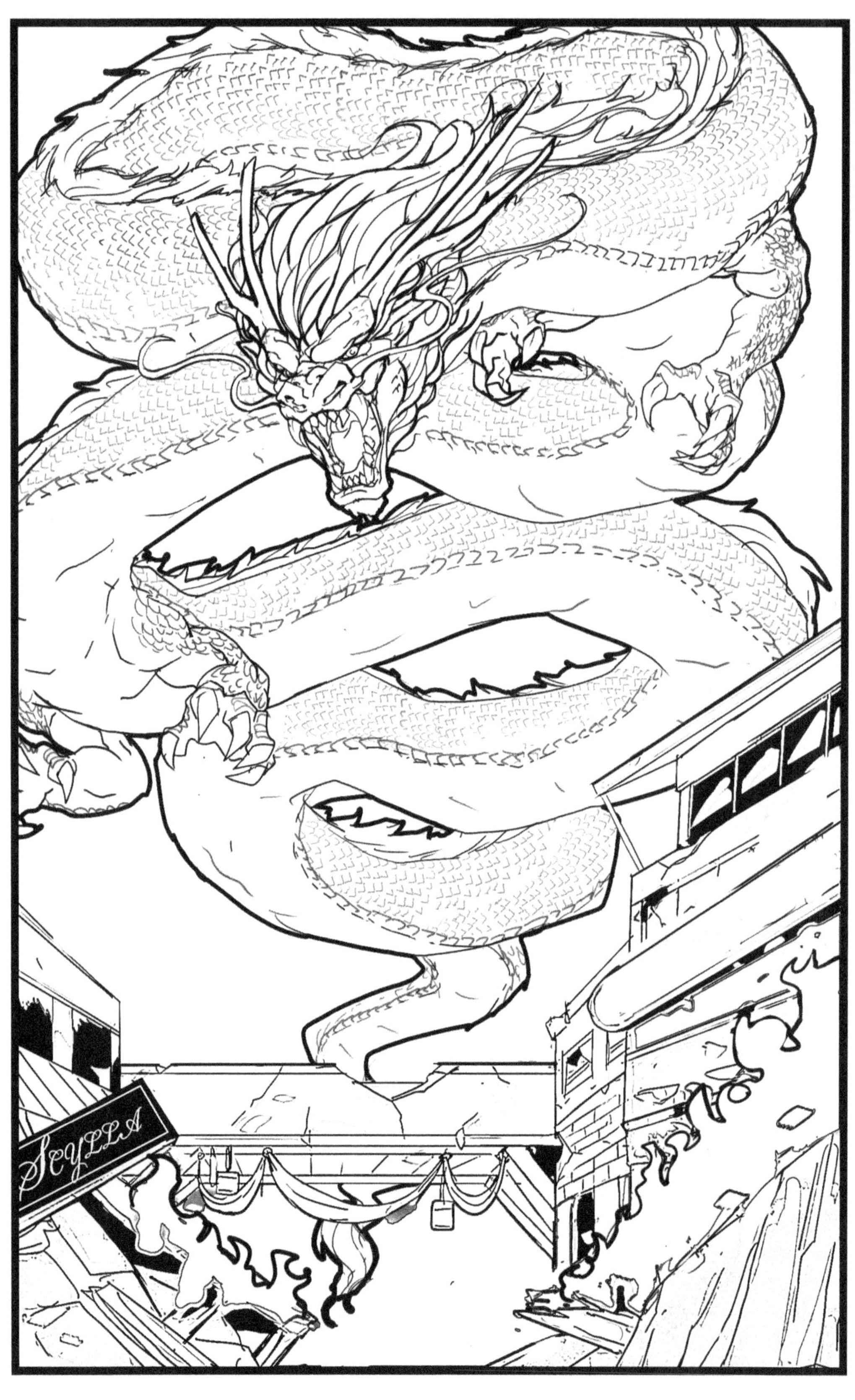

SEITADI

DRAKES

SIREN'S CURSE

Y I T A W L N B O R I S D K F V I L D V X K A
Q M Q Z N J Y W A O T W E A V U V N E W L W W
B Y A H L A K K N D K K G R R T H L E I D J Q
J S W T U R E E N Y I O M A U G N S Q A R F E
F T O T H C W R X P N N Z W X J B L L E K O L
B I L E L A H W D I J M A Z J S N T O O I C P
Y Q N Z O D L T A C X S V R Z F E W M B C E M
A U W X S I C A L G U Q S D A S N I T D T E E
O E L O T A D L S I N O P I E E T A H D W Z T
X H E Q P M O T R I G L M V L S I P S R I D S
A E V M D E I A X S A Q M B E T Y J Z Y T P R
R R S X T A M O O S N D M L S G A N H A Y R E
H B L W W D C R L E K L E P T O K N L D U D T
K S G V M O F M N R J C J U G O S S P I P R E
G D Q T D W R T C T B J M G N S E E W U D R M
N R C Y G S K B A S Z J E G O N U C R N M I E
C L O U D S D U M I T V P T A W D I J B A E D
I Z F Z R L X X A M D P N F J L S N I Z N K X
K I R W V E J A U H C A D S K T K U E S Z O R
B F F A B S N C S R S D B F I Z G Z E H R U L
R D H Y Z B R W R Z G E N E E N W S W W U O I
P P E J C Y O N P R I M E W A R R I O R K Z O
E S N O R E C A M E V O R G T N A D R E V L L

- ADINA
- ALTESE
- ARCADIA MEADOWS
- ATLIS
- CELESTIMO
- CLOUDS
- CYON
- DEMETERS TEMPLE
- DRYAD
- FAGONIA
- GENEEN
- IONE
- KEIR
- KLEPTO
- MACERON
- MARIUS
- MISTRESS
- MYSTIQUE HERBS
- ORIEL
- PRIME WARRIOR
- PURIST
- SANTOS
- SERU
- THALASIA
- VERDANT GROVE

SIREN'S CURSE

1. R Y E L ________

2. U S E R C __________

3. I V N D E __________

4. I G N A V __________

5. K L A S U __________

6. P M U S L __________

7. S E R I N __________

8. A A L E C R ____________

9. L G E U R I ____________

10. L S E E E N ____________

11. L O I S M L A ______________

12. O N R L A J U ______________

13. M R A H K A M ______________

14. A L I A V I S ______________

15. G W D I N E D ______________

16. C A I P N R A I ________________

17. E I A S S C O N N __________________

18. I E R R T Y P A N __________________

19. K I D A A M C R G ________ __________

20. W A D A D S O O L N ____________________

21. E N P Q U H E M Y N __________ __________

22. S L M O S N A F A I L ____________ __________

23. G E V A S M I L I G L A __________ ______________

24. E G E M K D N I L T R A H ______________ ____________

25. N N E L S T A E S D E I C C ____________________ ________

SIREN'S CURSE

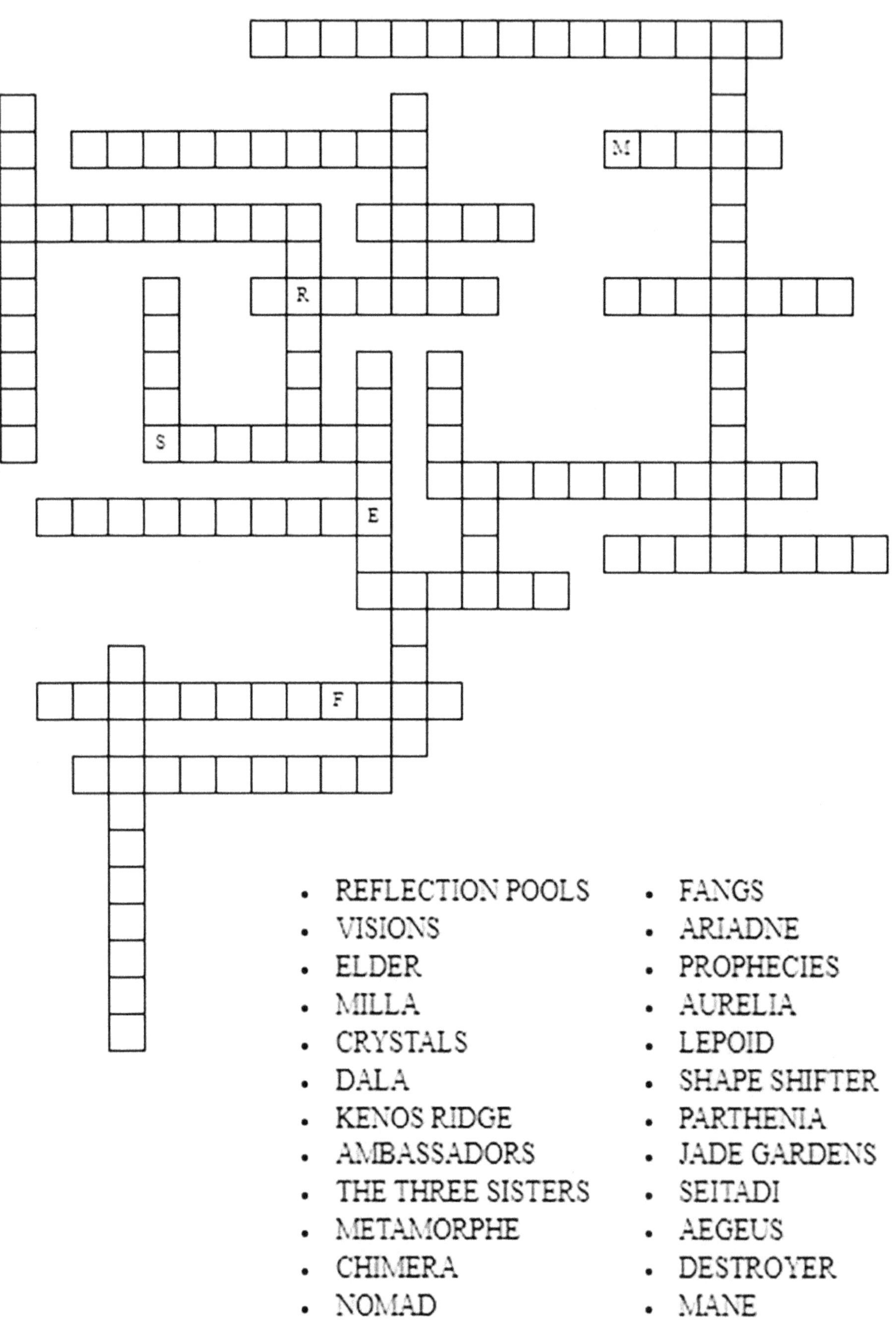

- REFLECTION POOLS
- VISIONS
- ELDER
- MILLA
- CRYSTALS
- DALA
- KENOS RIDGE
- AMBASSADORS
- THE THREE SISTERS
- METAMORPHE
- CHIMERA
- NOMAD
- FANGS
- ARIADNE
- PROPHECIES
- AURELIA
- LEPOID
- SHAPE SHIFTER
- PARTHENIA
- JADE GARDENS
- SEITADI
- AEGEUS
- DESTROYER
- MANE

HUNTED

THE ATLIS CHRONICLES BOOK 1

BY KRYS FENNER

Thalasia surveyed the barren wasteland in front of her. It was arid and dusty, completely desolate. Nothing but one empty home after another caught her eye. This couldn't be where her vision meant to take her. The portal she'd gone through led her to one set of ruins after another. How was she supposed to find a young siren here? Tucking her wings back and a strand of blue hair behind her ear, she stepped farther into the quiet village. While many stone huts still stood, others were piles of rubbish that resembled rotting animal carcasses.

What happened to this place? Was she too late to save the girl? Or was it merely one small piece of a puzzle she couldn't see? There had to be some way to find out. Thalasia lingered near the remnants of a house and peered through the grime-covered window as best she could. Layer upon layer of sand coated the furniture, at least what she could make out. Turning toward the village center, she called out, "Hello?"

It was probably stupid, but her only other option was to fly overhead. That might not give her more information than what lay before her. Not that it seemed to matter. The farther she trekked through the village remnants, the more apparent it all became. This place was utterly deserted. She could call out until she croaked, but no one would respond. As she approached the town's edge, Thalasia glanced toward the scorching sun.

It neared midday. None of the homes in this village shielded her from anything. Thalasia took off into the air, leaving it behind. She had to find someplace safe to stay for the night; then, she could start fresh in the morning. As she flew overhead, she scanned the sea of sand below, searching for any sign of life. Nothing. The vast, bone-dry basin offered her nothing except the heat beating down on her wings.

Gods, how long had she been in the sky? Eyeing the sun's position, she guesstimated at least a couple of hours. If only she could determine how far she'd gotten since departing the village. It all looked the same. Her body wasn't made for this kind of terrain. Unable to hold flight any longer, she landed with the grace of a peacock. Her talons scraped across the sand as her feet hit the ground. Her wings had dried out from the thick heat. Usually, she kept the siren appearance because it made her look like less of a threat. In this weather, she didn't think it benefited her.

Thalasia wiped the sweat from her brow, and with the flick of her hand, she adjusted her overall appearance to look human. She wiggled her toes in her leather boots, rolled her wingless shoulders, and wrapped a scarf over her head and around her mouth. Damn, that felt good. Now, if she could locate civilization somewhere in this realm of endless rolling foothills, that would be great.

The day wore on, but she'd gotten no closer to another village. Bahalah had to have something to offer her. Thalasia's gaze flicked briefly to the sun. It would set soon, she needed to find shelter somewhere. Her knowledge of this realm was limited. There was no telling what creatures wandered these dunes throughout the night. Halting her steps, she took a moment to settle her ragged breaths and scan her surroundings. Her eyes landed on another dune, except it was off somehow. Not that she could immediately determine how. Only one way to find out. She strode in that direction.

The closer she got to the bramble, the easier it became to discern that something lay beneath it. Perhaps a small cavern. However, it could be more extensive with the dune than her initial assessment. It offered shelter and a place to hide from whatever she might cross at night. Thalasia took a few minutes as she carefully navigated through the twisted shrubbery and into the cave. It was dark, but she could see well enough. Humans didn't have her eyesight. She slipped her backpack from her shoulders. It usually appeared as a small bag hung from a belt loop, but she'd seen people carry this in the human world.

Thalasia dug out a flashlight and turned it on, not that it lasted. "Damn it," she muttered as she smacked it against her palm. Gods, it would be so easy to summon light into her hand. Except humans couldn't do that either. Did this realm even have humans? She needed to scour the book before hitting a jump point. Grumbling under her breath, Thalasia located a fresh set of batteries, changed them, and got the flashlight up and running.

Shrugging her closed backpack onto her shoulders, she stepped farther into the cave. Thalasia scanned for any strange creature lurking about. This might make an excellent place to settle overnight. The flashlight's beam didn't reach too far, but it was enough as she swung it from one cavern wall to the other.

A flutter rippled through the air. Her ears twitched. Something was here, not that she could see what with the light. It hadn't attacked her; that didn't mean it wasn't dangerous. Thalasia turned off the flashlight and inserted it into the back pocket of her jeans. Much better. Just in case, she discreetly settled her hand on the blade's hilt tucked into her belt.

Surveying the walls, she noted slight changes in their coloration and formation. It might help her locate whatever hid in the cavern and watched her. Thalasia ran her fingers down the jagged edges of the stone barrier. It was nearby, but how close? "I know you're there. I'm not here to hurt you." Although it was the truth, none of them ever initially believed her. Not that she understood why. She didn't look threatening, did she? No matter. She had to figure out what had happened to this place. The success of her mission depended on it. Thalasia skimmed the wall as she walked forward.

Still nothing. No subtle movements for her ears to pick up. No differentiation of color against the walls that she observed. One slight flutter and she'd know which way to look. "I'm here to help, but the longer you hide, the less reason I have to trust you want life to improve."

The sound of paws thudding against the sand reached her. Thalasia stopped. It wasn't too far away. "Damn it," she muttered. Some creature must've picked up her scent like a damn bloodhound. Slipping her backpack from her shoulders, she removed the illusion and tied the velvet bag to her belt loop. She scanned the cavern. There had to be a way to cover her smell. She'd fight it if she knew what it was and how to kill it. And whatever hid here wasn't any damn help.

Sand covered the cavern floor, above it as well. As much as she hated to give some of her abilities away like this, there was no choice. Summoning her power, she shifted the terrain, pushed more grains toward the entrance, and coated her body in it. Gods, this sucked. She flattened her back against the wall.

Something launched forward with a mighty flap of its wings, clearing her scent from the cave, then it trapped her with its wings. Powerful appendages secured her arms and pressed into her body, the edge sealing over her mouth. "Stay quiet. Be still." With a few more flaps of its free wing, the sand intermingled with dust as it wafted toward the opening to create a cover. The cavern would appear nonexistent from the outside.

What the fuck was this thing? She'd seen some doozies in her life, all fifteen years, but nothing like *this*. It had fur. At least it appeared to have fur. Hard to tell with all the bandages. It wasn't a mummy, considering how it barked out orders. She would've responded *no shit* if it hadn't covered her mouth with its silky-smooth wings. Yep, not a mummy. Those things couldn't fly. She'd never encountered one.

This creature was unlike anything she'd ever seen before. This realm seemed to contain a lot of that. And it made the situation difficult if they had to escape for any reason. Did it really think her mouth was a problem? Like she needed it to...enchant? Internally groaning, Thalasia pressed her head back against the hard stone. *For fuck's sake, please don't tell me you sent me somewhere full of witches and warlocks.* No response. As if she expected less. Yeah, the gods could give her visions, but a conversation was always out of the question.

The sands shifted, and the earth quaked as the beast outside lumbered toward the cavern. The grit kicked up in its wake and rained down, spraying them. It snorted and chuffed. Its heated breath and strands of viscous saliva projected into the confined space, bathing them in its pungent stench.

Thalasia remained still and kept her breaths shallow, which was easier said than done with this thing holding her in place, especially as its feathered antennae tickled her exposed skin. She gazed at the creature just outside the cavern as best she could. Dear gods! It had no eyes, a barbed tail, and it was enormous. Despite all her abilities in her arsenal, she had no clue what would destroy the massive beast. Between what she and the thing pressed against her had done, it hopefully proved enough to keep the animal from further trailing their scent. Her gaze flicked toward the back of the cavern. There was no discernible exit, which meant they'd have to create one if it came down to it. Yeah, a great place to hide.

Listening intently, it sounded like the animal moved away from the entrance. Thalasia scrunched her nose as she drank in the sight of the unidentified, fuzzy creature in front of her. It reminded her of something, but she couldn't quite put her finger—oh! A moth. Except it was much bigger than an ordinary moth. More human-sized. Taller than her, and she hadn't yet hit five feet. Still, it looked strange. That was saying something, as she had invisible wings.

"I'm going to release you. I advise you to put your weapon away." It gently peeled its wing.

Weapon? What the fuck was it talking about? Thalasia tilted her head. "You mean my knife?" Taking her cue from the creature, she kept her voice low. It knew more about that beast than she did. "What was that thing?"

The moth-thing eased back, suspicion coloring its expression. Despite missing its arms, it was light on its feet. As it touched down on the sandstone, the sand barely shifted to acknowledge its weight. The wings, which dropped over its shoulders like a tattered cloak, stirred the sand with dust in the cramped hollow. "A knife is a weapon in the right hands." It dipped its chin toward the cavern's entrance. "You're a sorceress; you should know."

"A sorceress?" She scoffed. "I've been called a lot of things but never a witch." With a slight shake of her head, Thalasia unwrapped the scarf from her face, stepped off the wall, and dropped the glamour hiding her blue feathered wings. Much better. "Would a sorceress offer to heal you?" While she hadn't immediately said something, the creature's missing limbs hadn't gone unnoticed. Though if it stuck to its belief, it would likely refuse her.

"You're siren...but...not." It wobbled briefly but quickly steadied its stance. "My wounds are long healed. The wrappings prevent the grit from burrowing between the creases of what remains. Unless you can regrow limbs... You should learn to lead with how you plan to help. It's more diplomatic, less *hostile*." The antennae emphasized the word. The moth-like creature paced the space.

"Not sure. Never tried to regrow limbs, but I could try." Easier to address that than its suggestion over her approach. Diplomacy didn't always work. In her experience, it usually landed her in more trouble. "As I don't exactly know what happened here, hard to say how I can help. So, how about we try this? You answer a question, and I'll answer one."

"First, we should take to the sky," it instructed. "Before the razor-tail catches your scent on the wind and resumes the hunt." Without waiting for an answer, the moth-thing skillfully tucked its wings, took off through the opening, and darted into the twilit sky of darkening blue.

"Sure, why not," Thalasia muttered as she rolled her eyes. At least it gave her one piece of information. Now, if she could just figure out how to kill the razor-tail. Taking a few steps forward, she spread her wings wide and launched after the creature.

SILENCING
THE SHAPE SHIFTER
PRISMA ISLE
5

MARKHAM & MINERVA

THE REAPER

ARMAN, ELISE, & MADDOX

DEVIN & RAINN

SILENCING THE SHAPE SHIFTER

A M B R O S I A M P M M R X J O K B Q P N B J H I

R M H X Y W G R W K I K B P M E L T I N G O O D T

Q O L O U T S N E C V K V V X L N C L U V O C E X

V E H X O D Q K E I D A X E C Y E E C X N K A V G

C M X C Q N N L C H N Z U F I N V A D E R S S I F

K X A P Q S W P F M X C K D Y R G Q Y K L G T N A

L K M K O S I F D A A Z A E R W N T K C U W A A O

Y V H A K F I J Y N D R K R Q E S M E W Z R D X F

E E M C E G K P A K F Z K Q N E Y K M K X H W M W

Q A Y M R Y M G G W O B R E J A D P B O O X V P L

H K G U M B O U U T E J K A T Z T M D I I C A O J

N U O F S L M K Y K J U M S V P G I Y Z G M R M H

B P Z B A Q L P W Q Z R O P D C L Q O B I W I C S

S L G U S L M I N J U A L J H E O A L N S S L R N

P T E E Z C L R G O M J G T H S A L C V F F L Y T

D V D Q V B O E Y H C G W K Z N O T V E D E I S B

S A U M O N N Y N P T D A T G W L Z H G B O A T J

H R U I S O X C G S Q N N R J X W K R G W O H A E

E I X N W A O H D Z T A I F D M L X P O D Y G L Q

P A Q E F F R F K S N A C N T E G J Q H G F Q S U

E W L R N O T V O G X L R L G U N H Y G E I L K Q

S U C V D F I J E T E D E S O Z B S H C M H E K O

P Z H A F K E R G C B P A R T H E N I A M U V T Y

Y D M C G J P T O R T U R E L N N D Y G A L V G Y

K M O K U W U V L F A D A R A H Y X D B D X H C B

ADARA	DEVINA	AMBROSIA	SPOURGIFF
BOOKS	GARDENS	CRYSTALS	VARILLIAH
DEATH	JOCASTA	INVADERS	MARKETPLACE
GEMMA	MELTING	PREGNANT	FALLEN STARS
HADES	MINERVA	LIGHTNING	YOUR MAJESTY
LOGAN	TORTURE	PARTHENIA	REINCARNATION
AUDREY			

SILENCING THE SHAPE SHIFTER

R S T A A O L	______________
A F T I H A	____________
T B S A E	__________
V C E A	________
A I A L H D	____________
E T D N I Y S	______________
S L E I E	__________
I G L L A A B R E	__________________
B T E R G E M	______________
V R G E E I L G L U L I A	____________ ______________
M F N O T S I A N R	____________________
A J H A	________
I A L Y R B R	______________

N A L N A L I I L ____________________

A G M B I C A G ___________ ______

E T I E G M N _______________

I A V G G L S L I E M A ___________ _______________

H N I T G ___________

E I P C E R _____________

Q U E N E ___________

T O S N S A _____________

T N R O H ___________

I W N S T ___________

H S O R E I S E W T ___________ ___________

N N I A I Z _____________

SILENCING THE SHAPE SHIFTER

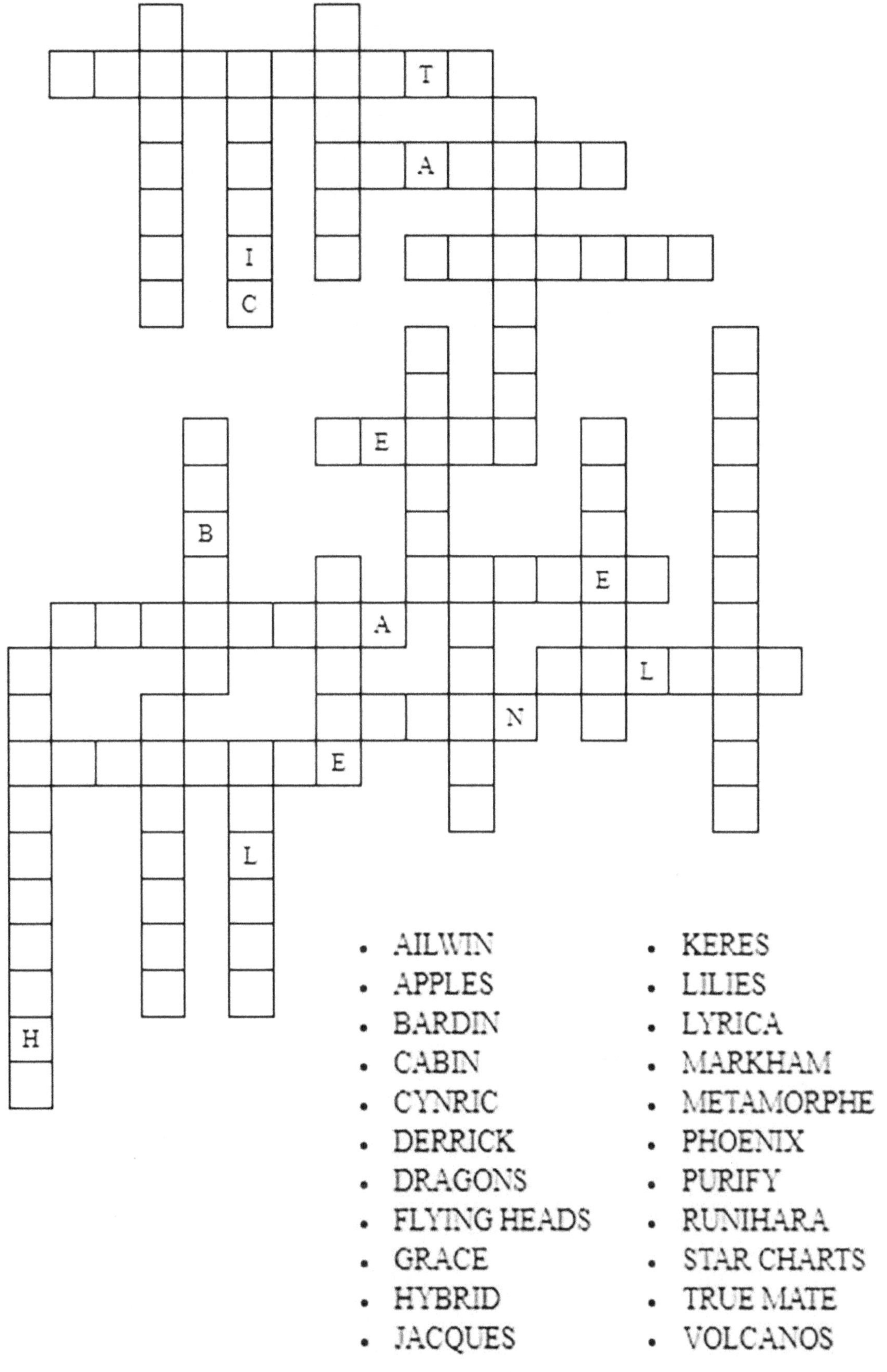

PRISMA ISLE

INSIDER'S GUIDE

LEX, MARISSA, & DORIAN

ELWIN & ANTONIA

ENGERAM & KEELIE

LEILAND, ANGELINA & ETHAN

MIDNIGHT & POTA

INSIDER'S GUIDE

```
O X W Y M D N H D B S O Q E M W O G A P P Y T G G
D K V G M W D C A S I U S C H I M E R A R T G G S
P U U M S R W A M N N Q K J R M V B X D M Q J S O
L E P I L O G U E S G H P E V A T H I A S O R S L
Q P L D Z X D K A C T E U U O B T C T E D E V V B
W Z Y N F V D W E M Z T L A D F S H E U T M F P L
E W P I O B W E K G T Z E I U G X Y P S G X C R E
G W A G P H L J M R O N C V N O V W I I N I E I P
T F V H N O S N Y O E J B N N A S S R L S W K E R
S A Q T C M G W R L N T K Z T J E H D D N Z P S E
A H A F I O B O E S O D G F C E I P H I I L U T C
T U E N G T T S B S M X W E R K R O W S B Z E E H
Y N U F B H N K M I O V F H G V I L E N G R B S A
R T I G C E N U B F F K T N L C E T D K O I S S U
S E B I E I B J K G Q E I C J S I L S C P S I E N
V R R U V R E R R N H K V X H R O U I M T F R I S
R U Q E Y Y L B O T Z L Y R P K F T K K W Y E P W
G R N Y F O A J V T L E C S C T N S E L U Y N H Z
G P F I J Y G O R E H A X F T A G H W N I P S I M
V I S D C B A A D E P E I X M R B A S I C W O N D
K N L O F O S R G N J S L M V D Y D C T U G U X A
D G A W Y Q R Y T S W J R O V C Y O S J T Y S R O
G A K X H W C N L R W V R G Q V L W M O W Q Q F T
V A K B O D F D S D W A R V E S E S C V T V I P N
Z J Q R T N C H I E F E L R O Y U P P L A R G K Y
```

- THE THREE SISTERS
- QUEEN SELENE
- CHIEF ELROY
- KING KIHRIG
- LEPRECHAUNS
- EPILOGUES
- MANTICORE
- PRIESTESS
- ANGELINA
- MIDNIGHT
- SEIPHINX
- UNICORNS
- BROTHEL
- CHIMERA
- DWARVES
- EVATHIA
- RICHTOR
- SHADOWS
- SPRITES
- HUNTER
- SATYRS
- SIRENS
- DEMON
- ELWIN
- NIMS

INSIDER'S GUIDE

1. E A U L I A R ______________

2. C T E R C A H R S A ____________________

3. C H B R O H T F C E E I __________ ______________

4. W N O N R C I G ________________

5. D S D A R Y ____________

6. E C D L I E A P N R I A R __________ ________________

7. E N G R A M E ______________

8. H A T N E __________

9. G L E U S I R ______________

10. X N J A O __________

11. L P E D I S O ______________

12. O D D M X A ____________

13. L M K R F O E ______________

14. A N H L I E P ______________

15. E I N E A S G P ________________

16. D E N E A E U E Q Y R __________ ____________

17. D E R ______

18. B E I S A S T S N T A __________ ____________

19. E L S I E E ____________

20. S U R E ________

21. I S R T S P F H E A H E S __________ ________________

22. S I G F O U R P F __________________

23. E A C E M H U A S R T S C T T N L ______ ______________ ______________

24. R S O T L L ____________

25. E K E Z ________

INSIDER'S GUIDE

CHROMETOURMALINE
CELEBRATION
ELDERARAGAR
QUEENDEVINA
CHIEFFRIGG
ENGAGEMENT
QUEENXANNA

TIMELINES
THALASIA
DRAGONS
LEILAND
MINERVA
SEITADI

SPECIES
ESCAPE
MARIUS
NYMPHS
SCENES
SHALLA

ATLIS
IVORY
LETTI
ROWAN
YOJAN
FAUN

BLOOD & BONDAGE

THE EMPYREAL DEN CHRONICLES
BOOK 1

BY B. NOIR & NIKKI HARAS

Hunter arrived at the brothel alone. Par for the course. Only on one other occasion had he brought someone along like he'd brought Maddox nine months ago. That male had needed something he couldn't find anywhere else. But he had found it here and seemed much happier for it, too.

Opening the door, Hunter headed inside and nodded to the dark-haired and red-headed females leaning against the wall. Maddox hadn't ever returned, not that he knew of, anyway. Just the one time. Hades, how could the male stand it? He couldn't see how once a year worked for anyone. If he just had sex once a year, he'd go insane.

Hunter crossed over to the receptionist's desk and dipped his chin to Shalla as he leaned a hip against the desk. Ivory had said she would meet him out here as soon as she ensured the new female was ready for him. "Evening. I am supposed to be meeting someone new tonight." A slight smirk played on his face as he set a bag of coins on the counter, enough for two hours. If he didn't enjoy this new female, or the session needed to end early, he'd get half back. This ensured they could continue if he wished, without the session being interrupted for more payment.

"Of course." Shalla collected the pouch and tucked it away inside her desk. "A few things before Ivory escorts you back. If things go well this session, the cost goes up by a hundred gold coins per hour for those that follow. While we allow some room for unexpected visits and overage, you must stick to whatever time you've scheduled. Understood?"

"Not a problem." It wasn't like he ever argued about any rules here, big or small. He needed, as much as he wanted, to come here; that was all there was to it. If this visit went well, he would gladly pay whatever he had to keep returning. And the money was no object, thanks to his side job that had filled his pockets, so to speak, over the years far more than being an Informant ever had. Reading between the lines when Ivory had told him a little about the female…he had a feeling he would not be disappointed, at the very least.

"Good."

Ivory sauntered toward them. She flashed Hunter a sultry smile and winked. "She's ready for you. If you'll come with me."

Hunter smirked down at her as he followed her down the hall. Gods, this must eat away at her. No matter how much Ivory smiled when telling him about a new female or taking him to their room for an introduction, he could tell that she always hated it. He had gone to her off and on for over twenty-five years. She was his backup. When things didn't go as planned with a new female, he returned to Ivory. Always. Not that he could even pinpoint why; it was just what he'd always done. She wasn't even great, just good enough. Barely.

Unlike the times when they had a session, Ivory didn't wrap her body around his, and he didn't put his arm around her. They just walked together. Anything else would have been entirely inappropriate, considering the circumstances. "And how are you doing today, sweetness?"

"I can't complain." She rounded the corner to the right, then led him down the next hallway on the left. "Her room is toward the back. She's one of our more exclusive workers."

"Good." Not that the thought entered his mind much or that he ultimately cared, but 'more exclusive' meant fewer dicks entered her pussy. Most of the females here were good at acting, but there had been a couple who had been obvious about being sloppy seconds over the years. Not on purpose, but that didn't change anything. And they hadn't lasted long—with him or the sanctum.

Ivory stopped in front of a black door. "Here we are." She leaned against the doorframe, stretching her arm above her head, and arched her back. "Though I'm positive you'll be happy with her…I'm always available if you ever change your mind."

Hunter slowly reached forward, allowing the fur on the back of his hand to brush against one of her breasts. The material of the covering she wore was so sheer that there wasn't a point in wearing anything at all. Even if she had on something else, he still would have seen how easily her nipples hardened. For fuck's sake, all he had to do was look at her, and she got wet. His smirk widened just the tiniest amount. Ivory would never truly be happy because she was continually chasing something that wouldn't ever happen for her—the perfect male. Or, perfect fuck, rather. Someone who would be exclusive only to her and raise her station here far above where she hoped to get. Someone that would make her feel like she was more than a paid whore. No one enjoyed her enough to give her all that, though, or it would have happened by now.

He placed his hand on the door above hers, leaned in, and whispered into her ear, "I know, sweetness, but that day will not be today. So, you should probably open the door." He flicked the tip of his tongue against her earlobe before straightening up again.

She pushed off the wall with a smile still plastered on her face. "Suit yourself." Opening the door, Ivory entered and stepped aside, revealing his new submissive.

As soon as he entered the room, a visible change came over his body. It was always like this; almost like, in moments of sexuality, he became a completely different person. No more teasing or playing around. No pet names or smiles. He became harder. Harsher. He had to be fully, totally, 100% in control. Fighting back, the word *no*, refusal to comply with a demand…that pissed him off, which was never good. Blood excited him, but he'd been as *good* as he could be to the females here. Not that he hadn't drawn it a time or two in the throes of ecstasy, but never anywhere near life-threatening. Never anything that wouldn't heal quickly. Once he drew blood on a female, they were done with him, and he had to move on to someone else, except for Ivory. He'd drawn blood on her once, and she'd ended it for a while, then allowed him to return after a few months.

No one could touch him during sex. He just couldn't stand it. It made his skin crawl. The sex he needed, craved, made him feel powerful, like a god. Gods took what they wanted without remorse. They didn't get punished. They didn't care about the disgusting things they'd done. They didn't have scars. They covered his body, head-to-toe, and this was the only time he couldn't handle being reminded they were there. Sex—sex like this—was the only time he forgot.

His gaze fell to the female kneeling on the floor in front of him in a perfect submissive pose. All she had on was a pair of sheer underwear, nothing else. Sometimes, he liked them to wear more when he started fucking his females, but it would do for the first time.

Fuck, just staring down at her had his cock thickening and hardening. He had to resist the urge to lick his lips as her scent invaded his nostrils. The subtle highlights in the female's hair shimmered beneath the flickering flames of the black candles along the wall. Her skin was utterly flawless. The swells of her breasts were ripe for the bite of his fangs. Her lips were plump and pouty, just slightly wet, begging to wrap themselves around his cock. He wanted to graze those slender hips of hers with his claws, grip them in his hands, and hold tight while he fucked the shit out of her.

It was exactly what he would do over the two hours that he'd paid to spend with her. "Does she know my preferences?" Once they started fucking, they could moan, cry out, and scream as much as they wanted, but no talking. 'Yes, Sir,' 'please' when they begged, their safe word, those kinds of things were acceptable. Other than that, it killed the mood.

"She's been apprised. The items that are allowed are hanging on the wall." Ivory gestured to the area to his right. "She will not move until you give her permission."

"Good. Leave us." Hunter stood there until Ivory left and the door closed behind her. He stared at the female for another moment, just drinking her in. "Get up."

She stood with great ease, her gaze still lowered and her hands at her side.

Hunter walked around her full circle, taking his time. "You will do," he said once he'd stopped in front of her again. Oh, but she would more than do. Hades, she was perfectly exquisite. He lifted her chin so their eyes met, unconsciously taking a moment to take in the minuscule nuances of their color—jade green with tiny flecks of yellow. The candlelight reflected in them almost made them appear gold for a moment. "My name is Hunter. When we are not playing, you may use my name. When we are playing, you will call me 'Sir.' Do you understand?"

"Yes, Sir."

Nothing outwardly showed on his face or in his demeanor, but internally he was practically drowning in pleasure already. Her voice was positively heavenly, the way 'Sir' just rolled off of her tongue. "I want your name and your safe word before we begin. I do not use gags, so you will always be able to use your safe word if you need to." Oh, but he hoped to all the gods she wouldn't need it. He had a feeling about her. This one…she would be perfection.

"I am called Nia. My safe word is blue, Sir."

Blue. A color she preferred, for sure. Nia wasn't her real name. Even if that wasn't a rule, he could just tell. She didn't state the name as if it *belonged* to her. It was just a name to be used. And as she'd said, it was what she was *called*. Likely, she hadn't even gotten to choose it for herself. Not using their real names kept the intimacy levels where they needed to stay. They weren't supposed to learn anything about one another. An unspoken rule he'd never broken. Even when massaging the females afterward, he didn't talk about himself. At all. Not really. He would brush their questions off with half-answers, never genuinely revealing anything about himself. That wasn't for any of them to know. They were playthings. Not friends. Not lovers.

That wasn't what this was about.

Which was why he came here. Anywhere else, the females expected things from him he wasn't prepared to give. They wanted *relationships*, something he would never be cut out for. He wasn't truly good for anyone and never would be. At least he recognized that about himself and spared the heartache to all those unsuspecting bitches around the isle. He gave a small internal laugh. Many were entranced by the draw, the danger of being with a male like him: a male who wore the Informant brand and survived Métamorphe under Markham. A savage who thrived on violence. If they knew what they were getting into when they came onto him, they'd tuck tail and run as if their lives depended on it. Because they did.

Only here, with rules, expectations, limits…this was the only place he could truly let himself go, and fuck like he really needed to. How long had he been standing here, staring at her? He was wasting coin; past time to get started. "Get on the bed."

"Yes, Sir."

Hunter stayed in his place as she climbed onto the bed. His tail twitched in anticipation while he waited for her to reach the center of the king-sized, four-poster bed. This bed was unique, and only in the rooms where a dominant was required, whether male or female. There were bars and shackles on the headboard and footboard, bars on top, and even a top-to-bottom 'X' on one side. A few other details to it ensured it functioned the way they needed.

Once she was comfortable, Hunter closed the distance and walked around to the top of the bed. "Extend your arms."

Nia followed his instruction without pause. This was a new room for him, just as the female was. They all had their own rooms, but the bed was basically the same as in the other rooms he frequented. Pulling up the chains with leather straps on the ends, he laid one on the mattress as he got the first one situated. Her wrists were so damn tiny, but the straps fit her perfectly. He adjusted the buckle tightly, but not enough to cut off her circulation, then did the same to the other. Hunter adjusted the chains so they were taut, her arms pulled straight above her head.

Already, his cock hardened more. Her scent alone had been enough to start that, then the view of her on the floor. Moving around to the foot of the bed, Hunter located the straps for her thighs before climbing up, first her right, then her left. He buckled the leather straps right above her knees, then pulled the chains tight, spreading her thighs wide. Then he just sat on his knees for a minute, gazing over her from head to toe. It differed from looking at the female for the first time in the submissive pose—a whole other experience.

His eyes passed over every dip and curve of her body. Each slight fluctuation in her skin tone. The slenderness of her neck. The way her collar bones jutted out just slightly. Not that she was malnourished at all, just small. Her body was completely hairless, just the way he liked. Female shape shifters had never attracted his attention, not that it was something he'd ever spoken out loud. She had a tiny, almost invisible dot right on her hip bone.

A barely noticeable scar on her waist. On her right arm was a tattoo of three intricately detailed roses. On her left leg was an ornate design of woven vines. Her rounded breasts were magnificent, nice and perky, the tips a bright pink.

This first session wouldn't get too rough or out of control. The first one with a female never did. She needed to feel him out, to see if she was comfortable with even the lowest levels of what he needed. And he needed to feel her out, too. Test her. Push the limits *just* a little before things escalated.

ANSWER KEY

PERFECTLY RECKLESS

```
F E R X M T G P D N N P L Y K V M P W C X A F
F V M F W I U U C X L Y P X L O V Y K G B J Z
E O G G T M G I M Y S E T N E M H S I N U P P
K L T Y A C P A U Y Q A O O N J K R Z Z W M F
I V M F O R H X S N X A N I T N I G Z E E Z O
O H X G I E C Z S V M S X T S C N D W C G C U
Z K N A N V Y G T U I P Q K O C G Q T A M U L
C K N I P A M B N X H L E I F S T T Z L J T P
W A L X O A L O P F Y W L O J Y Q Q C P E D F
O E Z J R L W L B X E J O A Q O X D Z T A N P
F N R A J O L B E F S E J M G I X C U E H N P
W O D J L I K A V I U N F T N E Q O I K Y V Y
S A I T H W W N F O R V O E R S E W T R B N M
Q Q B A R R I E R R U B O G W E A C T A R N K
V I K K L Y N E G A E H A N D M B M S M I U T
O S U E L D E R W N P T T G B Y Y M L K D K Y
B Z L A B Z P I J I G D A R K Q D N E I O T P
U D H R Y H N O S V W Z O W U E N A P G Y C L
O M P V R I I O T E D S J E G N A Y H S L M S
D Q M O R W B S B D I B E B U X P L J L G M N
P L R U E Z A Y C A G N M B L N D H D T I U N
H B Y H E A C Z H S I N G I N G N H L K Y A R
N X D E V O L E B X F D J O T R U E M A T E T
```

- ADARA
- AMBROSIA
- BARRIER
- BELOVED
- CABIN
- CIPRIANA
- DAHLIA
- DEVINA
- ELDER
- FELINE
- GABRIELLA
- GEMBERT
- HYBRID
- KING
- LEO
- LOVE
- MARKETPLACE
- MIGASVILLAGE
- MYQUEEN
- PHOENIX
- PUNISHMENT
- SANTOS
- SINGING
- TRUEMATE
- WATERFALL

PERFECTLY RECKLESS

1. R A M A A	A M A R A
2. T N S G A A R O A S R	A R R O G A N T A S S
3. R I G E B D	B R I D G E
4. H C Z A	C H A Z
5. Y S R U C	C Y R U S
6. A E D L E I N	D E L E N I A
7. S A H R N D O E I R G F T	D R A G O N S H I F T E R
8. A I A F G O N	F A G O N I A
9. F R T I N I G H G	F I G H T R I N G
10. A G I V N	G A V I N
11. O G E N S S M E T	G E M S T O N E S
12. S D H E A	H A D E S

14. N A L O G — L O G A N

15. D D X A O M — M A D D O X

16. R M H A T P E O M E — M E T A M O R P H E

17. I A S N A L O M S L F — M O S I N A   F A L L S

18. A A I P E N R T H — P A R T H E N I A

19. P E R A T I N R Y — P T E R Y R I N A

20. A I C C R F E S I — S A C R I F I C E

21. N E R I S — S I R E N

22. E T S R E E H U O — T R E E H O U S E

23. S L A I V A I — V A S I L I A

24. H H Y S G U R N E S I O — Y O U R   H I G H N E S S

25. N Z A N I I — Z I N N I A

PERFECTLY RECKLESS

DIMINUTIVEBEACH

ARMAN

MARKHAM

PIERCE

CROWSSKULLTRAIL

MOON

SHAPESHIFTER

MYSTIQUEHERBS

CANNON

INFORMANT

FELIX

GUILER

GALENUS

BRAND

DERRICK

LYRICA

LILLIANNA

THEFOURMUSES

TWINS

BEAR

EVAN

AILWIN

SABINA

GEMMA

ZANCLESROCK

CHAOTIC TRANQUILITY

W V D C A N E T E I X P M Y E X A N D E R V V I
P J S X W A E U M A J O O E Y T L S K U E A D I
Z A W D M Z F I H D M S K W T D A X K O E I O X
F O D H K U A Q P F K X E H O A W L D L T L S Z
L B Y M U W D D Z V X U N T H F M L O X C W L B
L D A H I N D I M P Z M I H F F L O E N Y I T F
E S D R O N T W W I G R A C E O H Q R L S N D Q
V X I C D P E I I S T L K M T D H T E P J B V K
D A F O K I H U N S Z P R E D I M U P A H F S J
R T E M Z X N U A G H N E Q O L B X Y U C E Q T
S N L H C F M E H R C F G Z P S D K W Y H L U L
O J W K M D B W S B E R I U M X Q E N S S X E L
N H O P A S P I R I T S O T C Z R S E R T G N N
R W O R C Y R A B I T E M A K A P I E S A R E Y
W G D O T O L C M P M A O Z M O L I Y L E M X D
G I W P U P V I W G H I Y T D L U X F M O L R L
Q X O H S X D T N K T T H C I A D U M H N Y E T
A M R E Q X N N R A L G I L B K O U N M A I L E
W Q K C F Y A A Y O I A D T D M S U D Y L M Z C
H S N Y R M M U C N T D B U A N V Q Y K H S X K
D G Z Y A Z H T N S H B I C K T V U Q M I O D Y
Y D F W D L U K N A Z Y R H I E M Y R O C K F Y
W S E E B M P Q N Q D B Q K F P A G E O T P K C
K F R B W K W R E F L E C T I O N P O O L S Y Q

- SET
- DUKE
- HOME
- MINE
- BEAST
- GRACE
- AILWIN
- BARDIN

- SUMMER
- TALONS
- XANDER
- HUNTING
- KAYLINA
- LILLIES
- MARKHAM
- MYROCK

- SPIRITS
- PROPHECY
- WOODWORK
- DAFFODILS
- NIGHTMARE
- CAMOUFLAGE
- METAMORPHE
- REFLECTIONPOOLS

CHAOTIC TRANQUILITY

1. T I S F A A A N	F A N T A S I A
2. Y B L L A U L	L U L L A B Y
3. M S E I N S E	N E M E S I S
4. P S R A T P T A E L	A P P L E T A R T S
5. T N H U R E	H U N T E R
6. R H S B E	H E R B S
7. N V I N E O S	V E N I S O N
8. K Y A A N	K A Y A N
9. N C R T M G I E A Y O N M E	M A T I N G C E R E M O N Y
10. D N K I M I L N	M I N D L I N K
11. S A R C S	S C A R S
12. R Y R E A A	R A Y A R E
13. U N N L E S T	T U N N E L S

14. B S I A N — B A S I N

15. E M U N Y E Q — M Y   Q U E E N

16. S D O G — G O D S

17. N I E C S R U R S E — S I R E N   C U R S E

18. I B L R A Y R — L I B R A R Y

19. T H R T S G N E — S T R E N G T H

20. E M R E D T E — D E M E T E R

21. G T A — T A G

22. I N I N Z — Z I N N I

23. C I T H A — C A I T H

24. R U S C Y — C Y R U S

25. T P G R N N A E — P R E G N A N T

CHAOTIC TRANQUILITY

REBEL TIDES

I E A Y J V C I A W R X V F S K K O S S I
G J Y N F Y I A X Q V M G E F C X E J T U
N N O E B H F N Y W I F N H X F I T J A T
T Q G X Y F F C N A S O E C Y R C F M I A
E T K U E W E M S K M H X L I U H A T R B
N Y M M I H L E A O E Z W A I E I X S W I
E H I A P L L E R N M E F E A X C F R A G
Q C S O H A E E P C T N P O I F A C D Y A
U I R S C R H R I R P I R E G I N A I T R
K P Y S O P B L N X E O C S R S E V N O M
E F L E J S L Y R S B C H O C J V V R H Y
Y D A T P O Q E E F X P H V R R I G N E P
Q R Z O R F P Y D C Y F C A P E L W G A O
I A V T X E E U S L N H P Z U P L H A V V
Z K S X E R R Y G O H P B H F N A O J E E
I E X K E R Z E R S Y E S R F E G A V N R
H S R V W W X E D S O P C C I V E T H J I
K A L W E N C H A N T R E S S D W Q T Z E
B I K T X A R W R O C Y N R I C G P I B X
S B U R M O T X B P J I P W T V E E O S B
N X F I D V P R C O L L A R I T O B E Y V

- ARMY
- BARKEEPER
- BRIDGE
- CHICANEVILLAGE
- COLLAR
- CYNRIC
- DRAKES
- ENCHANTRESS
- FAIRIES
- FELIX
- GLYPHS
- GUILER
- INNKEEPER
- KEY
- LEPRECHAUN
- MACERON
- MANTICORE
- PHEROMONES
- PROPHECY
- REGINA
- SCALES
- SILVEREYES
- STAIRWAYTOHEAVEN
- TROLL
- VERIE

REBEL TIDES

1. BTAAENSIST	SAINT BEAST
2. SECNACLORKZ	ZANCLES ROCK
3. OFLCSADDNLOU	LAND OF CLOUDS
4. GMIAC	MAGIC
5. AERV	VERA
6. ENGTER	REGENT
7. UELAAIR	AURELIA
8. KYMEESPTL	SKY TEMPLE
9. GELINSRDGONTS	GOLDEN STRINGS
10. TODHNABRUE	EARTHBOUND
11. EYLR	LYRE
12. GDLDIE	GILDED
13. AOIHDNUM	HUMANOID

14. O S E P N R I R — P R I S O N E R

15. M E I A R K — M E R A K I

16. O H E C N — E N O C H

17. Y A K O K E C E O K A J R — K A R A O K E J O C K E Y

18. S E E T A S R F H P I H — S H A P E S H I F T E R

19. R W I U C A T L R S K L L O — C R O W S K U L L T R A I L

20. V E I N I H C U B T E D I A M — D I M I N U T I V E B E A C H

21. L D U O C C T R O U — C L O U D C O U R T

22. K O B O — B O O K

23. S A H L I T A A — T H A L A S I A

24. E A F E S R T H — F E A T H E R S

25. T A Y T A L C S — C A T A L Y S T

REBEL TIDES

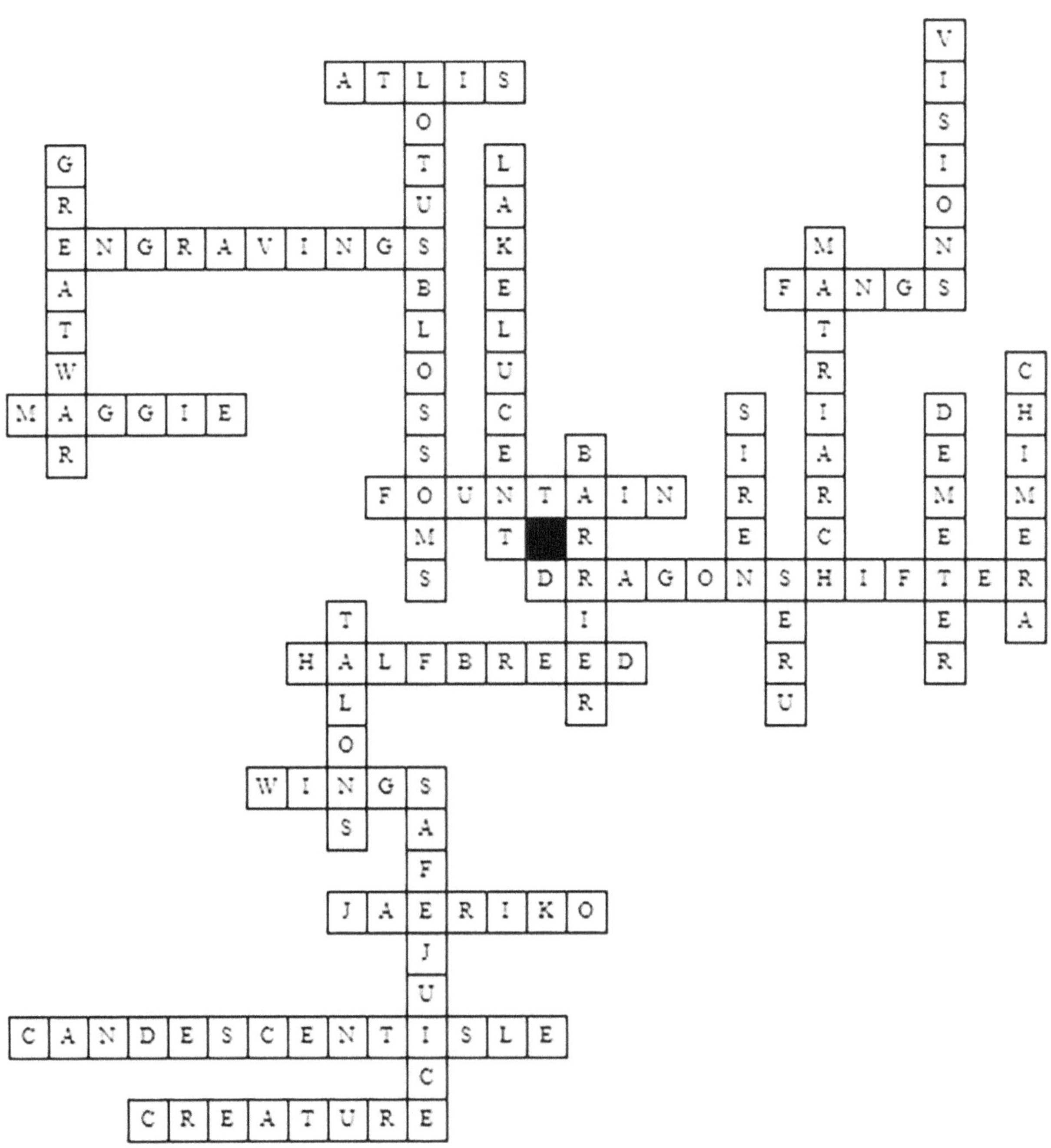

ATLIS
VISIONS
LOTUSBLOSSOMS
GREATWAR
LAKELUCENT
ENGRAVINGS
MATRIARCH
FANGS
CHIMERA
MAGGIE
SIREN
DEMETER
BARRIER
FOUNTAIN
DRAGONSHIFTER
SERU
TALONS
HALFBREED
WINGS
SAFEJUICE
JAERIKO
CANDESCENTISLE
CREATURE

SIREN'S CURSE

- ADINA
- ALTESE
- ARCADIAMEADOWS
- ATLIS
- CELESTIMO
- CLOUDS
- CYON
- DEMETERSTEMPLE
- DRYAD
- FAGONIA
- GENEEN
- IONE
- KEIR
- KLEPTO
- MACERON
- MARIUS
- MISTRESS
- MYSTIQUEHERBS
- ORIEL
- PRIMEWARRIOR
- PURIST
- SANTOS
- SERU
- THALASIA
- VERDANTGROVE

SIREN'S CURSE

1. R Y E L	L Y R E
2. U S E R C	C U R S E
3. I V N D E	D E V I N
4. I G N A V	G A V I N
5. K L A S U	K L A U S
6. P M U S L	P L U M S
7. S E R I N	S I R E N
8. A A L E C R	A R A C E L
9. L G E U R I	G U I L E R
10. L S E E E N	S E L E N E
11. L O I S M L A	A L L I M O S
12. O N R L A J U	J O U R N A L
13. M R A H K A M	M A R K H A M

14. A L I A V I S — V A S I L I A

15. G W D I N E D — W E D D I N G

16. C A I P N R A I — C I P R I A N A

17. E I A S S C O N N — A S C E N S I O N

18. I E R R T Y P A N — P T E R Y R I N A

19. K I D A A M C R G — D A R K   M A G I C

20. W A D A D S O O L N — S A N D A L W O O D

21. E N P Q U H E M Y N — N Y M P H   Q U E E N

22. S L M O S N A F A I L — M O S I N A   F A L L S

23. G E V A S M I L I G L A — M I G A S   V I L L A G E

24. E G E M K D N I L T R A H — E M E R A L D   K N I G H T

25. N N E L S T A E S D E I C C — C A N D E S C E N T   I S L E

SIREN'S CURSE

SILENCING THE SHAPE SHIFTER

ADARA	DEVINA	AMBROSIA	SPOURGIFF
BOOKS	GARDENS	CRYSTALS	VARILLIAH
DEATH	JOCASTA	INVADERS	MARKETPLACE
GEMMA	MELTING	PREGNANT	FALLENSTARS
HADES	MINERVA	LIGHTNING	YOURMAJESTY
LOGAN	TORTURE	PARTHENIA	REINCARNATION
AUDREY			

SILENCING THE SHAPE SHIFTER

RSTAAOL	A L A S T O R
AFTIHA	A T I F A H
TBSAE	B E A S T
VCEA	C A V E
AIALHD	D A H L I A
ETDNIYS	D E S T I N Y
SLEIE	E L I S E
IGLLAABRE	G A B R I E L L A
BTERGEM	G E M B E R T
VRGEEILGLULIA	G U I L E R V I L L A G E
MFNOTSIANR	I N F O R M A N T S
AJHA	J A H A
IALYRBR	L I B R A R Y

NALNALIIL	L I L L I A N N A
AGMBICAG	M A G I C B A G
ETIEGMN	M E E T I N G
IAVGGLSLIEMA	M I G A S V I L L A G E
HNITG	N I G H T
EIPCER	P I E R C E
QUENE	Q U E E N
TOSNSA	S A N T O S
TNROH	T H O R N
IWNST	T W I N S
HSOREISEWT	W H I T E R O S E S
NNIAIZ	Z I N N I A

SILENCING THE SHAPE SHIFTER

			M				B										
	S	T	A	R	C	H	A	R	T	S							
			R		Y		R				V						
			K		N		D	R	A	G	O	N	S				
			H		R		I				L						
			A		I		N		J	A	C	Q	U	E	S		
			M		C						A						
									L		N					F	
									Y		O					L	
				H			K	E	R	E	S		P			Y	
				Y					I				H			I	
				B					C				O			N	
				R			G		A	P	P	L	E	S		G	
	R	U	N	I	H	A	R	A		U			N			H	
M				D			A			R		L	I	L	I	E	S
E			D				C	A	B	I	N		X			A	
T	R	U	E	M	A	T	E			F						D	
A			R		I					Y						S	
M			R		L												
O			I		W												
R			C		I												
P			K		N												
H																	
E																	

INSIDER'S GUIDE

- THE THREE SISTERS
- QUEEN SELENE
- CHIEF ELROY
- KING KIHRIG
- LEPRECHAUNS
- EPILOGUES
- MANTICORE
- PRIESTESS
- ANGELINA
- MIDNIGHT
- SEIPHINX
- UNICORNS
- BROTHEL
- CHIMERA
- DWARVES
- EVATHIA
- RICHTOR
- SHADOWS
- SPRITES
- HUNTER
- SATYRS
- SIRENS
- DEMON
- ELWIN
- NIMS

INSIDER'S GUIDE

Scrambled	Answer
1. E A U L I A R	A U R E L I A
2. C T E R C A H R S A	C H A R A C T E R S
3. C H B R O H T F C E E I	C H I E F O B R E C H T
4. W N O N R C I G	C R O W N I N G
5. D S D A R Y	D R Y A D S
6. E C D L I E A P N R I A R	E L D E R C I P R I A N A
7. E N G R A M E	E N G E R A M
8. H A T N E	E T H A N
9. G L E U S I R	G U I L E R S
10. X N J A O	J A X O N
11. L P E D I S O	L E P O I D S
12. O D D M X A	M A D D O X
13. L M K R F O E	M E R F O L K

14. A N H L I E P — N E P H A L I

15. E I N E A S G P — P E G A S I N E

16. D E N E A E U E Q Y R — Q U E E N D Y E E R A

17. D E R — R E D

18. B E I S A S T S N T A — S A I N T B E A S T S

19. E L S I E E — S E E L I E

20. S U R E — S E R U

21. I S R T S P F H E A H E S — S H A P E S H I F T E R S

22. S I G F O U R P F — S P O U R G I F F

23. E A C E M H U A S R T S C T T N L — T H E S C A R L E T S A N C T U M

24. R S O T L L — T R O L L S

25. E K E Z — Z E K E

INSIDER'S GUIDE

ABOUT THE AUTHORS

Krys Fenner, also known as **Brigit Rosé**—like the wine, not the flower, has been infinitely passionate about writing and helping people for as long as she can remember. Having already published nine books, she avidly works on multiple series from social issues to paranormal romance. While she loves everything she writes, she's genuinely excited for the two series she'll be co-authoring over the coming year. Krys received an Associate of Arts in Psychology, a Bachelor of Arts in Creative Writing, and is currently working on a Master's degree. When she isn't writing, she's spending time with her three fur babies, Bones, Luna, and Lola.

Follow on social media:

Twitter: @FennerKrys
Facebook: @KrysFenner
Pinterest: @krysfenner3
Website: **https://brigitrose.wordpress.com/**

Instagram: @romance_brigit_rose
Pinterest: @krysfenner3
Website: https://kbfennerrose.com

Nikki Haras has had a passion for writing since she was a small child. She used paper and pen/pencil, an old typewriter from her mother, and her father's computer in her youth. These days, random scraps of paper, dozens of notebooks, a notepad app on her phone, her beloved laptop. When she's not immersing herself in her fantasy worlds, she's a full-time mom of three children, two fur babies, Luna and Lucifer, and one aquatic baby, Giovanni. She will use whatever means necessary to get the words down that swirl inside her head; breathe life into the characters who demand to tell their stories. Nikki has been previously published in two charity anthologies that are no longer in print, but if you check out her website, you will find a compilation of all her anthology pieces in an e-book collection for $0.99.

Follow on social media:

Facebook: https://www.facebook.com/Nikki-Haras-100804125556236
Website: **https://nikkiharas1988.wixsite.com/mysite**

www.ingramcontent.com/pod-product-compliance
Lightning Source LLC
Chambersburg PA
CBHW080918190726
48293CB00011B/2689

* 9 7 8 1 9 5 5 1 0 6 1 9 1 *